HAROLD PINTER

Betrayal

First published in 1978 by Eyre Methuen Limited

Revised paperback edition first published in 1980 by Methuen London Ltd

First published in 1991 by Faber & Faber Ltd,
Bloomsbury House, 74–77 Great Russell Street, London WC1B 3DA

Paperback edition reset with small amendments first published in 2013

This Modern Classics edition first published in 2018

Typeset by Country Setting, Kingsdown, Kent CT14 8ES
Printed by CPI Group (UK) Ltd, Croydon, CR0 4YY

A CIP record for this book is available from the British Library

ISBN 978-0-571-33878-8

2 4 6 8 10 9 7 5 3

Foreword

Harold's magical play *Betrayal* has a special place in my heart because it was the first play he wrote when we were together. Before we met, I had admired his work, including his screenplays such as *Accident*, and then conceived a passion for *Old Times*. I was on the *Evening Standard*'s drama panel at the time, and voted strongly for *Old Times* to win the 1971 award for best play: it was defeated by a play called *Butley* by Simon Gray – which was directed by Harold.

After we met, Harold spent the next year writing poetry, mainly to me, which I imagined fondly was the way our lives would go for ever. I was therefore completely unprepared for the state of restless happiness into which he was suddenly plunged when seized with the inspiration to write *Betrayal*. Afterwards I discovered that this happiness, and this restlessness day and night until the journey was over, was characteristic of his writing mode. From outside, it appeared to be quite unlike any other state of mind he experienced. Comparisons to his ecstasy over England winning Test matches are not relevant, because there he was for ever the spectator; here he was right in the middle of the enchanted maze. I shall never forget the experience of witnessing first-hand this act of creation. And I shall always adore the play!

Antonia Fraser,
August 2017

Introduction

Betrayal is one of Harold Pinter's most popular, resonant and formally perfect plays. It was turned into a highly successful film in 1983 with Jeremy Irons, Patricia Hodge and Ben Kingsley. It has had four major, subtly different London revivals in the last twenty years. In 2013 it became a hot Broadway ticket in a Mike Nichols production starring Daniel Craig, Rachel Weisz and Rafe Spall. It even in 1997 inspired an episode of the TV comedy hit, *Seinfeld*, which, like Pinter's play, ran in reverse chronological order. If you include the various radio versions – one of them featuring the author himself – and the countless regional and international revivals, you could argue that few Pinter plays have reached so many people.

Yet it is fascinating to recall that *Betrayal* did not enjoy instant acclaim: coolly received at first, it has gone on, not unlike *The Birthday Party*, to be accepted as a vital part of the modern canon and it is worth examining why. There was, however, no doubt on the part of its initial interpreters that they were dealing with something special. Peter Hall directed the first production at the National Theatre in November 1978 and in his *Diaries* he records his excitement. He immediately understood that it was infinitely more than a study of adultery amongst the London literati. His entry for 20 October 1978 reads:

> It is an advance for Harold this play. The tension builds up at an enormous rate. It's not fanciful to think

> of Mozart. From my point of view, there's the same precision of means, the same beauty, the same lyricism and the same sudden descents into pain which are quickly over because of a healthy sense of the ridiculous. A strange comparison I know. But it's there.

Hall went on to express his delight in the performances of Michael Gambon, Penelope Wilton and Daniel Massey. But, although rehearsals went well, the first night was a more than usually fraught affair. The reason was that the National Theatre was in the midst of an industrial dispute, with unofficial strikes constantly threatened. There was no guarantee that the first performance of *Betrayal* would go ahead or that it might not be abruptly curtailed at any point. As Peter Hall wrote in his *Diaries*, 'The tension on this first night was the most cruel of my experience.'

The reviews the next morning, my own in the *Guardian* included, were chilly to the point of hostility: the general complaint was that Pinter, the master of ambiguity, was simply offering variations on the old theme of the eternal triangle. Benedict Nightingale in the *New Statesman* came to the play's rescue by stating that its theme was not 'the sexual aspects of adultery' but 'the politics of betrayal'. Peter Jenkins in the *Spectator*, in reference to its reverse time-scheme, also called it 'a technical tour de force' and Martin Esslin in *Plays and Players* claimed 'this is a new Pinter and yet the old Pinter, the Pinter of oblique and indirect approach, the Pinter of hidden subtleties and deep layers of gradually emerging meaning'.

What many of us failed to realise at the time, however,

was just what Pinter was up to. It was partly because in 1978, at a period of economic crises and mainland IRA bomb threats, we were conditioned to expect drama to deal with public issues rather than private affairs. We were also guilty of stock responses to Pinter's work. Having been trained to see Pinter's work as enigmatic, puzzling and elliptical – what, after all, is the fate of Stanley at the end of *The Birthday Party* or Ruth at the climax of *The Homecoming*? – we were taken aback at the seeming explicitness of *Betrayal*. The truth is, of course, that *Betrayal* is itself as profound, shaded and multi-faceted as anything Pinter has written.

Even the first scene, a pub reunion between Emma and Jerry, who were once lovers, is fraught with meaning. Emma, who now runs a thriving art gallery, seems poised, assured, controlled; Jerry, in contrast, is tentative, uncertain, gauche. Emma, you feel, has moved on while Jerry is enslaved by the past. Emma, speaking of a chance trip to Kilburn where they once had an adulterous love nest, casually says, 'I thought of you the other day.' Jerry later observes, 'I don't need to *think* of you', as if his whole being were still permeated by her presence. But, for all her fortitude, Emma is not armour-plated. She reveals her shock on learning the previous evening of the serial infidelity of her husband, Robert. Jerry, if anything, seems even more wounded than Emma by the news of Robert's, his best friend's, clandestine affairs. He is also duped by Emma into believing that she only told Robert of their own relationship the previous evening.

In that one scene Pinter introduces, with masterful economy, a number of key themes: female resilience, male insecurity, the inequality of passion, the power of memory. Above all, he captures the labyrinthine nature of deceit. And this is a topic that he explores in the succeeding eight scenes which take us back in time, from 1977 to 1968 and to Jerry's first rapturous declaration of his love. Both temporally and thematically the whole play pivots on an extraordinary scene in a Venice hotel room in 1973 where Robert learns, by chance, of Emma's affair with Jerry. The perfect symmetry of Pinter's play is demonstrated by the fact that, just before the crucial revelation, Emma and Robert are chatting about a new novel she is reading. Robert considers, though she doesn't, that its theme is betrayal, of which he slightingly remarks, 'Oh . . . not much more to say on that subject, really, is there?'

The irony is, of course, that Pinter's play itself reveals that the subject is inexhaustible. On one level, the play is about the complex mathematics of sexual and emotional deceit. But it is also about self-betrayal. It is vital to the play that Jerry is an agent and Robert a publisher who talk of authors as their 'boys' and of the literary business as if it were an endless production line. Pinter is at pains to point out that, as undergraduates, they were both editors of poetry magazines and consumed by a love of literature for its own sake. Jerry used to write long letters about Ford Madox Ford and Robert about Yeats, the ultimate poet of loss and decline. As we see them, they have not just grown into super-efficient literary middlemen but symbols of all those who betray their youthful idealism for a life of comfort and ease.

As Peter Hall said, *Betrayal* represents for Pinter an advance rather than a retreat. Without sacrificing his instinct for ambiguity, he writes a play that is immediately accessible. He creates in Emma a woman who – again in Hall's words – is 'enchanting, vigorous, life-enhancing with a keen appetite for life, a good intellect, a marvellous sense of humour'. It is also worth pointing out that *Betrayal* represents a significant landmark in Pinter's personal and professional life. His previous play, *No Man's Land* in 1975, had an existential bleakness that reflected the reclusive unhappiness of his life at that time. After that, his marriage to Vivien Merchant broke up and he forged a new, loving and long-lasting relationship with Antonia Fraser. In the short-term, domestic disruption prevented Pinter writing anything but by the time he and Fraser moved into her Holland Park home in 1977 he was able to contemplate a new play; and that sense of liberation is in *Betrayal*.

The initial notion that the play was a simplistic study of adultery has also been knocked on the head by an excellent series of revivals. All Pinter's plays are susceptible to reinterpretation and are defined by the personality of their performers; and that is as true of *Betrayal* as any other. Each time I see the play, I take something new from it. Peter Hall's 2003 revival, which came to the Duchess from the Theatre Royal, Bath, was most striking for Janie Dee's Emma. I'd never quite realised before how much Emma treats the Kilburn refuge less as love nest than as a surrogate home and even pines for a more permanent relationship than Jerry is willing to provide. Dee also exploited the play's structure to show Emma shedding guilt and stress, like a snake sloughing its skin, as the action moved backwards in time.

In Roger Michell's 2007 revival at the Donmar Warehouse it was Samuel West's Robert who seemed the pivotal figure. At first, West appeared to view the fluctuations of adultery with the cold indifference of the semi-detached. But West gradually let you see that Robert adopts a sardonic mask in order to conceal a broken heart. At the London lunch Robert has with Jerry, shortly after his discovery of the affair with Emma, West desperately sought to hide his wounds under tight-lipped smiles: even the cravat he suddenly sported suggested a man affecting a Wildean bravura.

Ian Rickson's 2011 production at the Comedy – now appropriately re-christened the Harold Pinter Theatre – went even further in bringing out the play's element of heartache. Although Emma is the survivor, there was a sadness to Kristin Scott Thomas as she bid farewell to Kilburn with its echoes of remembered passion. As Douglas Henshall's Jerry lightly touched her fingers in the pub scene, he seemed painfully aware of what he too had lost. And, after the revelations of the Venetian hotel scene, Ben Miles's Robert abandoned his studied insouciance to first hurl a bed-cover at Emma's head and then lean across to wipe away her tears.

Betrayal, in short, is a play that yields up new secrets with each successive reading or viewing. Sometimes it seems to be about the peculiar clubby camaraderie of the Anglo-Saxon male: at other times about the defiant resourcefulness of women in the face of emotional crisis. But what pervades it at all times is a sense of the headlong joys and exquisite torments of love and of the endless circularity of deception. A play that had a difficult baptism and was at first grotesquely misunderstood has endured for forty years and will, I suspect, last as long as human beings continue to betray both each other and themselves.

Michael Billington, August 2017

Cheryl Campbell
Bill Nighy
Marion Shaw

Betrayal was first produced by the National Theatre, London, on 15 November 1978, with the following cast:

EMMA	Penelope Wilton
JERRY	Michael Gambon
ROBERT	Daniel Massey
A WAITER	Artro Morris
A BARMAN	Glenn Williams

Directed by Peter Hall
Designed by John Bury

The play was produced at the Almeida Theatre, London, on 17 January 1991, with the following cast:

EMMA	Cheryl Campbell
JERRY	Bill Nighy
ROBERT	Martin Shaw
A WAITER	Stefano Gressieux

Directed by David Leveaux
Designed by Mark Thompson

It was produced in the Lyttelton auditorium of the National Theatre, London, on 24 November 1998, with the following cast:

EMMA	Imogen Stubbs
JERRY	Douglas Hodge
ROBERT	Anthony Calf
A WAITER	Arturo Venegas

Directed by Trevor Nunn
Designed by Es Devlin

It was produced by the Peter Hall Company at the Theatre Royal, Bath, on 9 July 2003, with the following cast:

EMMA	Janie Dee
JERRY	Aden Gillett
ROBERT	Hugo Speer
A WAITER	James Supervia

Directed by Peter Hall
Designed by John Gunter

This production transferred to the Duchess Theatre, London, on 8 October 2003.

It was produced at the Donmar Warehouse, London, on 21 July 2007, with the following cast:

EMMA	Dervla Kirwan
JERRY	Toby Stephens
ROBERT	Samuel West
A WAITER	Paul Di Rollo

Directed by Roger Michell
Designed by William Dudley

It was produced at the Harold Pinter Theatre (formerly Comedy Theatre), London, on 16 June 2011, with the following cast:

EMMA	Kristin Scott Thomas
JERRY	Douglas Henshall
ROBERT	Ben Miles
A WAITER	John Guerrasio

Directed by Ian Rickson
Designed by Jeremy Herbert

Characters

Emma

Jerry

Robert

In 1977 Emma is thirty-eight
Jerry and Robert are forty.

The play can be performed without an interval
or with an interval after Scene Four.

BETRAYAL

1977

SCENE ONE

Pub. 1977. Spring.

Noon.

EMMA *is sitting at a corner table.* JERRY *approaches with drinks, a pint of bitter for him, a glass of wine for her.*

He sits. They smile, toast each other silently, drink.

He sits back and looks at her.

JERRY

Well . . .

EMMA

How are you?

JERRY

All right.

EMMA

You look well.

JERRY

Well, I'm not all that well, really.

EMMA

Why? What's the matter?

JERRY

Hangover.

He raises his glass.

Cheers.

He drinks.

How are you?

EMMA

I'm fine.

She looks round the bar, back at him.

Just like old times.

JERRY

Mmm. It's been a long time.

EMMA

Yes.

Pause.

I thought of you the other day.

JERRY

Good God. Why?

She laughs.

JERRY

Why?

EMMA

Well, it's nice, sometimes, to think back. Isn't it?

JERRY

Absolutely.

Pause.

How's everything?

EMMA

Oh, not too bad.

Pause.

Do you know how long it is since we met?

JERRY

Well I came to that private view, when was it – ?

EMMA

No, I don't mean that.

JERRY

Oh you mean alone?

EMMA

Yes.

JERRY

Uuh . . .

EMMA

Two years.

JERRY

Yes, I thought it must be. Mmnn.

Pause.

EMMA

Long time.

JERRY

Yes. It is.

Pause.

How's it going? The Gallery?

EMMA

How do you think it's going?

JERRY

Well. Very well, I would say.

EMMA

I'm glad you think so. Well, it is actually. I enjoy it.

JERRY

Funny lot, painters, aren't they?

EMMA

They're not at all funny.

JERRY

Aren't they? What a pity.

Pause.

How's Robert?

EMMA

When did you last see him?

JERRY

I haven't seen him for months. Don't know why. Why?

EMMA

Why what?

JERRY

Why did you ask when I last saw him?

EMMA

I just wondered. How's Sam?

JERRY

You mean Judith.

EMMA

Do I?

JERRY

You remember the form. I ask about your husband, you ask about my wife.

EMMA

Yes, of course. How is your wife?

JERRY

All right.

Pause.

EMMA

Sam must be . . . tall.

JERRY

He is tall. Quite tall. Does a lot of running. He's a long distance runner. He wants to be a zoologist.

EMMA

No, really? Good. And Sarah?

JERRY

She's ten.

EMMA

God. I suppose she must be.

JERRY

Yes, she must be.

Pause.

Ned's five, isn't he?

EMMA

You remember.

JERRY

Well, I would remember that.

Pause.

EMMA

Yes.

Pause.

You're all right, though?

JERRY

Oh . . . yes, sure.

Pause.

EMMA

Ever think of me?

JERRY

I don't need to think of you.

EMMA

Oh?

JERRY

I don't need to *think* of you.

Pause.

Anyway I'm all right. How are you?

EMMA

Fine, really. All right.

JERRY

You're looking very pretty.

EMMA

Really? Thank you. I'm glad to see you.

JERRY

So am I. I mean to see you.

EMMA

You think of me sometimes?

JERRY

I think of you sometimes.

Pause.

I saw Charlotte the other day.

EMMA

No? Where? She didn't mention it.

JERRY

She didn't see me. In the street.

EMMA

But you haven't seen her for years.

JERRY

I recognised her.

EMMA

How could you? How could you know?

JERRY

I did.

EMMA

What did she look like?

JERRY

You.

EMMA

No, what did you think of her, really?

JERRY

I thought she was lovely.

EMMA

Yes. She's very . . . She's smashing. She's thirteen.

Pause.

Do you remember that time . . . oh God it was . . . when you picked her up and threw her up and caught her?

JERRY

She was very light.

EMMA

She remembers that, you know.

JERRY

Really?

EMMA

Mmnn. Being thrown up.

JERRY

What a memory.

Pause.

She doesn't know . . . about us, does she?

EMMA

Of course not. She just remembers you, as an old friend.

JERRY

That's right.

Pause.

Yes, everyone was there that day, standing around, your husband, my wife, all the kids, I remember.

EMMA

What day?

JERRY

When I threw her up. It was in your kitchen.

EMMA

It was in your kitchen.

Silence.

JERRY

Darling.

EMMA

Don't say that.

Pause.

It all . . .

JERRY

Seems such a long time ago.

EMMA

Does it?

JERRY

Same again?

He takes the glasses, goes to the bar. She sits still. He returns, with the drinks, sits.

EMMA

I thought of you the other day.

Pause.

I was driving through Kilburn. Suddenly I saw where I was. I just stopped, and then I turned down Kinsale Drive and drove into Wessex Grove. I drove past the house and then stopped about fifty yards further on, like we used to do, do you remember?

JERRY

Yes.

EMMA

People were coming out of the house. They walked up the road.

JERRY

What sort of people?

EMMA

Oh . . . young people. Then I got out of the car and went up the steps. I looked at the bells, you know, the names on the bells. I looked for our name.

Pause.

JERRY

Green.

Pause.

Couldn't see it, eh?

EMMA

No.

JERRY

That's because we're not there any more. We haven't been there for years.

EMMA

No we haven't.

Pause.

JERRY

I hear you're seeing a bit of Casey.

EMMA

What?

JERRY

Casey. I just heard you were . . . seeing a bit of him.

EMMA

Where did you hear that?

JERRY

Oh . . . people . . . talking.

EMMA

Christ.

JERRY

The funny thing was that the only thing I really felt was irritation, I mean irritation that nobody gossiped about us like that, in the old days. I nearly said, now look, she may be having the occasional drink with Casey, who cares, but she and I had an affair for seven years and none of you bastards had the faintest idea it was happening.

Pause.

EMMA

I wonder. I wonder if everyone knew, all the time.

JERRY

Don't be silly. We were brilliant. Nobody knew. Who ever went to Kilburn in those days? Just you and me.

Pause.

Anyway, what's all this about you and Casey?

EMMA

What do you mean?

JERRY

What's going on?

EMMA

We have the occasional drink.

JERRY

I thought you didn't admire his work.

EMMA

I've changed. Or his work has changed. Are you jealous?

JERRY

Of what?

Pause.

I couldn't be jealous of Casey. I'm his agent. I advised him about his divorce. I read all his first drafts. I persuaded your husband to publish his first novel. I escort him to Oxford to speak at the Union. He's my . . . he's my boy. I discovered him when he was a poet, and that's a bloody long time ago now.

Pause.

He's even taken me down to Southampton to meet his Mum and Dad. I couldn't be jealous of Casey. Anyway it's not as if we're having an affair now, is it? We haven't seen each other for years. Really, I'm very happy if you're happy.

Pause.

What about Robert?

Pause.

EMMA

Well . . . I think we're going to separate.

JERRY

Oh?

EMMA

We had a long talk . . . last night.

JERRY

Last night?

EMMA

You know what I found out . . . last night? He's betrayed me for years. He's had . . . other women for years.

JERRY

No? Good Lord.

Pause.

But we betrayed him for years.

EMMA

And he betrayed me for years.

JERRY

Well I never knew that.

EMMA

Nor did I.

Pause.

JERRY

Does Casey know about this?

EMMA

I wish you wouldn't keep calling him Casey. His name is Roger.

JERRY

Yes. Roger.

EMMA

I phoned *you*. I don't know why.

JERRY

What a funny thing. We were such close friends, weren't we? Robert and me, even though I haven't seen him for a few months, but through all those years, all the drinks, all the lunches . . . we had together, I never even gleaned . . . I never suspected . . . that there was anyone else . . . in his life but you. Never. For example, when you're with a fellow in a pub, or a restaurant, for example, from time to time he pops out for a piss, you see, who doesn't, but what I mean is, if he's making a crafty telephone call, you can sort of sense it. Well, I never did that with Robert. He never made any crafty telephone calls in any pub I was ever with him in. The funny thing is that it was me who made the calls – to you, when I left him boozing at the bar. That's the funny thing.

Pause.

When did he tell you all this?

EMMA

Last night. I think we were up all night.

Pause.

JERRY

You talked all night?

EMMA

Yes. Oh yes.

Pause.

JERRY

I didn't come into it, did I?

EMMA

What?

JERRY

I just –

EMMA

I just phoned you this morning, you know, that's all, because I . . . because we're old friends . . . I've been up all night . . . the whole thing's finished . . . I suddenly felt I wanted to see you.

JERRY

Well, look, I'm happy to see you. I am. I'm sorry . . . about . . .

EMMA

Do you remember? I mean, you do remember?

JERRY

I remember.

Pause.

EMMA

You couldn't really afford Wessex Grove when we took it, could you?

JERRY

Oh, love finds a way.

EMMA

I bought the curtains.

JERRY

You found a way.

EMMA

Listen, I didn't want to see you for nostalgia, I mean what's the point? I just wanted to see how you were. Truly. How are you?

JERRY

Oh what does it matter?

Pause.

You didn't tell Robert about me last night, did you?

EMMA

I had to.

Pause.

He told me everything. I told him everything. We were up . . . all night. At one point Ned came down. I had to take him up to bed, had to put him back to bed. Then I went down again. I think it was the voices woke him up. You know . . .

JERRY

You told him everything?

EMMA

I had to.

JERRY

You told him everything . . . about us?

EMMA

I had to.

Pause.

JERRY

But he's my oldest friend. I mean, I picked his own daughter up in my own arms and threw her up and caught her, in my kitchen. He watched me do it.

EMMA

It doesn't matter. It's all gone.

JERRY

Is it? What has?

EMMA

It's all all over.

She drinks.

1977 Later

SCENE TWO

Jerry's House. Study. 1977. Spring.

JERRY *sitting.* ROBERT *standing, with glass.*

JERRY

It's good of you to come.

ROBERT

Not at all.

JERRY

Yes, yes, I know it was difficult . . . I know . . . the kids . . .

ROBERT

It's all right. It sounded urgent.

JERRY

Well . . . You found someone, did you?

ROBERT

What?

JERRY

For the kids.

ROBERT

Yes, yes. Honestly. Everything's in order. Anyway, Charlotte's not a baby.

JERRY

No.

Pause.

Are you going to sit down?

ROBERT

Well, I might, yes, in a minute.

Pause.

JERRY

Judith's at the hospital . . . on night duty. The kids are . . . here . . . upstairs.

ROBERT

Uh – huh.

JERRY

I must speak to you. It's important.

ROBERT

Speak.

JERRY

Yes.

Pause.

ROBERT

You look quite rough.

Pause.

What's the trouble?

Pause.

It's not about you and Emma, is it?

Pause.

I know all about that.

JERRY

Yes. So I've . . . been told.

ROBERT

Ah.

Pause.

Well, it's not very important, is it? Been over for years, hasn't it?

JERRY

It is important.

ROBERT

Really? Why?

JERRY *stands, walks about.*

JERRY

I thought I was going to go mad.

ROBERT

When?

JERRY

This evening. Just now. Wondering whether to phone you. I had to phone you. It took me . . . two hours to phone you. And then you were with the kids . . . I thought I wasn't going to be able to see you . . . I thought I'd go mad. I'm very grateful to you . . . for coming.

ROBERT

Oh for God's sake! Look, what exactly do you want to say?

Pause.

JERRY *sits.*

JERRY

I don't know why she told you. I don't know how she could tell you. I just don't understand. Listen, I know you've got . . . look, I saw her today . . . we had a drink . . . I haven't seen her for . . . she told me, you know, that you're in trouble, both of you . . . and so on. I know that. I mean I'm sorry.

ROBERT

Don't be sorry.

JERRY

Why not?

Pause.

The fact is I can't understand . . . why she thought it necessary . . . after all these years . . . to tell you . . . so suddenly . . . last night . . .

ROBERT

Last night?

JERRY

Without consulting me. Without even warning me. After all, you and me . . .

ROBERT

She didn't tell me last night.

JERRY

What do you mean?

Pause.

I know about last night. She told me about it. You were up all night, weren't you?

ROBERT

That's correct.

JERRY

And she told you . . . last night . . . about her and me. Did she not?

ROBERT

No, she didn't. She didn't tell me about you and her last

night. She told me about you and her four years ago.

Pause.

So she didn't have to tell me again last night. Because I knew. And she knew I knew because she told me herself four years ago.

Silence.

JERRY

What?

ROBERT

I think I will sit down.

He sits.

I thought you knew.

JERRY

Knew what?

ROBERT

That I knew. That I've known for years. I thought you knew that.

JERRY

You thought I knew?

ROBERT

She said you didn't. But I didn't believe that.

Pause.

Anyway I think I thought you knew. But you say you didn't?

JERRY

She told you . . . when?

ROBERT

Well, I found out. That's what happened. I told her I'd found out and then she . . . confirmed . . . the facts.

JERRY

When?

ROBERT

Oh, a long time ago, Jerry.

Pause.

JERRY

But we've seen each other . . . a great deal . . . over the last four years. We've had lunch.

ROBERT

Never played squash though.

JERRY

I was your best friend.

ROBERT

Well, yes, sure.

JERRY *stares at him and then holds his head in his hands.*

Oh, don't get upset. There's no point.

Silence.

JERRY *sits up.*

JERRY
Why didn't she tell me?

ROBERT
Well, I'm not her, old boy.

JERRY
Why didn't you tell me?

Pause.

ROBERT
I thought you might know.

JERRY
But you didn't know for *certain*, did you? You didn't *know*!

ROBERT
No.

JERRY
Then why didn't you tell me?

Pause.

ROBERT

Tell you what?

JERRY

That you knew. You bastard.

ROBERT

Oh, don't call me a bastard, Jerry.

Pause.

JERRY

What are we going to do?

ROBERT

You and I are not going to do anything. My marriage is finished. I've just got to make proper arrangements, that's all. About the children.

Pause.

JERRY

You hadn't thought of telling Judith?

ROBERT

Telling Judith what? Oh, about you and Emma. You mean she never knew? Are you quite sure?

Pause.

No, I hadn't thought of telling Judith, actually. You

don't seem to understand. You don't seem to understand that I don't give a shit about any of this. It's true I've hit Emma once or twice. But that wasn't to defend a principle. I wasn't inspired to do it from any kind of moral standpoint. I just felt like giving her a good bashing. The old itch . . . you understand.

Pause.

JERRY

But you betrayed her for years, didn't you?

ROBERT

Oh yes.

JERRY

And she never knew about it. Did she?

ROBERT

Didn't she?

Pause.

JERRY

I didn't.

ROBERT

No, you didn't know very much about anything, really, did you?

Pause.

JERRY

No.

ROBERT

Yes you did.

JERRY

Yes I did. I lived with her.

ROBERT

Yes. In the afternoons.

JERRY

Sometimes very long ones. For seven years.

ROBERT

Yes, you certainly knew all there was to know about that. About the seven years of afternoons. I don't know anything about that.

Pause.

I hope she looked after you all right.

Silence.

JERRY

We used to like each other.

ROBERT

We still do.

Pause.

I bumped into old Casey the other day. I believe he's having an affair with my wife. We haven't played squash for years, Casey and me. We used to have a damn good game.

JERRY

He's put on weight.

ROBERT

Yes, I thought that.

JERRY

He's over the hill.

ROBERT

Is he?

JERRY

Don't you think so?

ROBERT

In what respect?

JERRY

His work. His books.

ROBERT

Oh his books. His art. Yes his art does seem to be falling away, doesn't it?

JERRY

Still sells.

ROBERT

Oh, sells very well. Sells very well indeed. Very good for us. For you and me.

JERRY

Yes.

ROBERT

Someone was telling me – who was it – must have been someone in the publicity department – the other day – that when Casey went up to York to sign his latest book, in a bookshop, you know, with Barbara Spring, you know, the populace queued for hours to get his signature on his book, while one old lady and a dog queued to get Barbara Spring's signature, on her book. I happen to think that Barbara Spring . . . is good, don't you?

JERRY

Yes.

Pause.

ROBERT

Still, we both do very well out of Casey, don't we?

JERRY

Very well.

Pause.

ROBERT

Have you read any good books lately?

JERRY

I've been reading Yeats.

ROBERT

Ah. Yeats. Yes.

Pause.

JERRY

You read Yeats on Torcello once.

ROBERT

On Torcello?

JERRY

Don't you remember? Years ago. You went over to Torcello in the dawn, alone. And read Yeats.

ROBERT

So I did. I told you that, yes.

Pause.

Yes.

Pause.

Where are you going this summer, you and the family?

JERRY

The Lake District.

1975

SCENE THREE
Flat. 1975. Winter.

JERRY *and* EMMA. *They are sitting.*

Silence.

JERRY
What do you want to do then?

Pause.

EMMA
I don't quite know what we're doing, any more, that's all.

JERRY
Mmnn.

Pause.

EMMA
I mean, this flat . . .

JERRY
Yes.

EMMA
Can you actually remember when we were last here?

JERRY

In the summer, was it?

EMMA

Well, was it?

JERRY

I know it seems –

EMMA

It was the beginning of September.

JERRY

Well, that's summer, isn't it?

EMMA

It was actually extremely cold. It was early autumn.

JERRY

It's pretty cold now.

EMMA

We were going to get another electric fire.

JERRY

Yes, I never got that.

EMMA

Not much point in getting it if we're never here.

JERRY

We're here now.

EMMA

Not really.

Silence.

JERRY

Well, things have changed. You've been so busy, your job, and everything.

EMMA

Well, I know. But I mean, I like it. I want to do it.

JERRY

No, it's great. It's marvellous for you. But you're not –

EMMA

If you're running a gallery you've got to run it, you've got to be there.

JERRY

But you're not free in the afternoons. Are you?

EMMA

No.

JERRY

So how can we meet?

EMMA

But look at the times you're out of the country. You're never here.

JERRY

But when I am here you're not free in the afternoons. So we can never meet.

EMMA

We can meet for lunch.

JERRY

We can meet for lunch but we can't come all the way out here for a quick lunch. I'm too old for that.

EMMA

I didn't suggest that.

Pause.

You see, in the past . . . we were inventive, we were determined, it was . . . it seemed impossible to meet . . . impossible . . . and yet we did. We met here, we took this flat and we met in this flat because we wanted to.

JERRY

It would not matter how much we wanted to if you're not free in the afternoons and I'm in America.

Silence.

Nights have always been out of the question and you know it. I have a family.

EMMA

I have a family too.

JERRY

I know that perfectly well. I might remind you that your husband is my oldest friend.

EMMA

What do you mean by that?

JERRY

I don't *mean* anything by it.

EMMA

But what are you trying to say by saying that?

JERRY

Jesus. I'm not *trying* to say anything. I've said precisely what I wanted to say.

EMMA

I see.

Pause.

The fact is that in the old days we used our imagination and we'd take a night and make an arrangement and go to an hotel.

JERRY

Yes. We did.

Pause.

But that was . . . in the main . . . before we got this flat.

EMMA

We haven't spent many nights . . . in this flat.

JERRY

No.

Pause.

Not many nights anywhere, really.

Silence.

EMMA

Can you afford . . . to keep it going, month after month?

JERRY

Oh . . .

EMMA

It's a waste. Nobody comes here. I just can't bear to think about it, actually. Just . . . empty. All day and night. Day after day and night after night. I mean the crockery and the curtains and the bedspread and everything. And the tablecloth I brought from Venice. (*Laughs.*) It's ridiculous.

Pause.

It's just . . . an empty home.

JERRY

It's not a home.

Pause.

I know . . . I know what you wanted . . . but it could never . . . actually be a home. You have a home. I have a home. With curtains, et cetera. And children. Two children in two homes. There are no children here, so it's not the same kind of home.

EMMA

It was never intended to be the same kind of home. Was it?

Pause.

You didn't ever see it as a home, in any sense, did you?

JERRY

No, I saw it as a flat . . . you know.

EMMA

For fucking.

JERRY

No, for loving.

EMMA

Well, there's not much of that left, is there?

Silence.

JERRY

I don't think we don't love each other.

Pause.

EMMA

Ah well.

Pause.

What will you do about all the . . . furniture?

JERRY

What?

EMMA

The contents.

Silence.

JERRY

You know we can do something very simple, if we want to do it.

EMMA

You mean sell it to Mrs Banks for a small sum and . . . and she can let it as a furnished flat?

JERRY

That's right. Wasn't the bed here?

EMMA

What?

JERRY

Wasn't it?

EMMA

We bought the bed. We bought everything. We bought the bed together.

JERRY

Ah. Yes.

EMMA *stands.*

EMMA

You'll make all the arrangements, then? With Mrs Banks?

Pause.

I don't want anything. Nowhere I can put it, you see. I have a home, with tablecloths and all the rest of it.

JERRY

I'll go into it, with Mrs Banks. There'll be a few quid, you know, so . . .

EMMA

No, I don't want any *cash*, thank you very much.

Silence. She puts coat on.

I'm going now.

He turns, looks at her.

Oh here's my key.

Takes out keyring, tries to take key from ring.

Oh Christ.

Struggles to take key from ring.
Throws him the ring.

You take it off.

He catches it, looks at her.

Can you just do it please? I'm picking up Charlotte from school. I'm taking her shopping.

He takes key off.

Do you realise this is an afternoon? It's the Gallery's afternoon off. That's why I'm here. We close every Thursday afternoon. Can I have my keyring?

He gives it to her.

Thanks. Listen. I think we've made absolutely the right decision.

She goes.

He stands.

1974

SCENE FOUR

Robert and Emma's House. Living room. 1974. Autumn.

ROBERT *pouring a drink for* JERRY. *He goes to the door.*

ROBERT

Emma! Jerry's here!

EMMA (*off*)

Who?

ROBERT

Jerry.

EMMA

I'll be down.

ROBERT *gives the drink to* JERRY.

JERRY

Cheers.

ROBERT

Cheers. She's just putting Ned to bed. I should think he'll be off in a minute.

JERRY

Off where?

ROBERT

Dreamland.

JERRY

Ah. Yes, how is your sleep these days?

ROBERT

What?

JERRY

Do you still have bad nights? With Ned, I mean?

ROBERT

Oh, I see. Well, no. No, it's getting better. But you know what they say?

JERRY

What?

ROBERT

They say boys are worse than girls.

JERRY

Worse?

ROBERT

Babies. They say boy babies cry more than girl babies.

JERRY

Do they?

ROBERT

You didn't find that to be the case?

JERRY

Uh . . . yes, I think we did. Did you?

ROBERT

Yes. What do you make of it? Why do you think that is?

JERRY

Well, I suppose . . . boys are more anxious.

ROBERT

Boy babies?

JERRY

Yes.

ROBERT

What the hell are they anxious about . . . at their age? Do you think?

JERRY

Well . . . facing the world, I suppose, leaving the womb, all that.

ROBERT

But what about girl babies? They leave the womb too.

JERRY

That's true. It's also true that nobody talks much about girl babies leaving the womb. Do they?

ROBERT

I am prepared to do so.

JERRY

I see. Well, what have you got to say?

ROBERT

I was asking you a question.

JERRY

What was it?

ROBERT

Why do you assert that boy babies find leaving the womb more of a problem than girl babies?

JERRY

Have I made such an assertion?

ROBERT

You went on to make a further assertion, to the effect that boy babies are more anxious about facing the world than girl babies.

JERRY

Do you yourself believe that to be the case?

ROBERT

I do, yes.

Pause.

JERRY

Why do you think it is?

ROBERT

I have no answer.

Pause.

JERRY

Do you think it might have something to do with the difference between the sexes?

Pause.

ROBERT

Good God, you're right. That must be it.

EMMA *comes in.*

EMMA

Hullo. Surprise.

JERRY

I was having tea with Casey.

EMMA

Where?

JERRY

Just around the corner.

EMMA

I thought he lived in . . . Hampstead or somewhere.

ROBERT

You're out of date.

EMMA

Am I?

JERRY

He's left Susannah. He's living alone round the corner.

EMMA

Oh.

ROBERT

Writing a novel about a man who leaves his wife and three children and goes to live alone on the other side of London to write a novel about a man who leaves his wife and three children –

EMMA

I hope it's better than the last one.

ROBERT

The last one? Ah, the last one. Wasn't that the one about the man who lived in a big house in Hampstead with his wife and three children and is writing a novel about – ?

JERRY (*to* EMMA)

Why didn't you like it?

EMMA

I've told you actually.

JERRY

I think it's the best thing he's written.

EMMA

It may be the best thing he's *written* but it's still bloody dishonest.

JERRY

Dishonest? In what way dishonest?

EMMA

I've told you, actually.

JERRY

Have you?

ROBERT

Yes, she has. Once when we were all having dinner, I remember, you, me, Emma and Judith, where was it, Emma gave a dissertation over the pudding about dishonesty in Casey with reference to his last novel. 'Drying Out.' It was most stimulating. Judith had to leave unfortunately in the middle of it for her night shift at the hospital. How is Judith, by the way?

JERRY

Very well.

Pause.

ROBERT

When are we going to play squash?

JERRY

You're too good.

ROBERT

Not at all. I'm not good at all. I'm just fitter than you.

JERRY

But why? Why are you fitter than me?

ROBERT

Because I play squash.

JERRY

Oh, you're playing? Regularly?

ROBERT

Mmnn.

JERRY

With whom?

ROBERT

Casey, actually.

JERRY

Casey? Good Lord. What's he like?

ROBERT

He's a brutally honest squash player. No, really, we haven't played for years. We must play. You were rather good.

JERRY

Yes, I was quite good. All right. I'll give you a ring.

ROBERT

Why don't you?

JERRY

We'll make a date.

ROBERT

Right.

JERRY

Yes. We must do that.

ROBERT

And then I'll take you to lunch.

JERRY

No, no. I'll take you to lunch.

ROBERT

The man who wins buys the lunch.

EMMA

Can I watch?

Pause.

ROBERT

What?

EMMA

Why can't I watch and then take you both to lunch?

ROBERT

Well, to be brutally honest, we wouldn't actually want a woman around, would we, Jerry? I mean a game of squash isn't simply a game of squash, it's rather more than that. You see, first there's the game. And then there's the shower. And then there's the pint. And then there's lunch. After all, you've been at it. You've had your battle. What you want is your pint and your lunch. You really don't want a woman buying you lunch. You don't actually want a woman within a mile of the place, any of the places, really. You don't want her in the squash court, you don't want her in the shower, or the pub, or the restaurant. You see, at lunch you want to talk about squash, or cricket, or books, or even women, with your friend, and be able to warm to your theme without fear of improper interruption. That's what it's all about. What do you think, Jerry?

JERRY

I haven't played squash for years.

Pause.

ROBERT

Well, let's play next week.

JERRY

I can't next week. I'm in New York.

EMMA

Are you?

JERRY

I'm going over with one of my more celebrated writers, actually.

EMMA

Who?

JERRY

Casey. Someone wants to film that novel of his you didn't like. We're going over to discuss it. It was a question of them coming over here or us going over there. Casey thought he deserved the trip.

EMMA

What about you?

JERRY

What?

EMMA

Do you deserve the trip?

ROBERT

Judith going?

JERRY

No. He can't go alone. We'll have that game of squash when I get back. A week, or at the most ten days.

ROBERT

Lovely.

JERRY (*to* EMMA)

Bye.

ROBERT *and* JERRY *leave.*

She remains still.

ROBERT *returns. He kisses her. She responds. She breaks away, puts her head on his shoulder, cries quietly. He holds her.*

1973

SCENE FIVE

Hotel Room. Venice. 1973. Summer.

EMMA *on bed reading.* ROBERT *at window looking out. She looks up at him, then back at the book.*

EMMA

It's Torcello tomorrow, isn't it?

ROBERT

What?

EMMA

We're going to Torcello tomorrow, aren't we?

ROBERT

Yes. That's right.

EMMA

That'll be lovely.

ROBERT

Mmn.

EMMA

I can't wait.

Pause.

ROBERT

Book good?

EMMA

Mmn. Yes.

ROBERT

What is it?

EMMA

This new book. This man Spinks.

ROBERT

Oh that. Jerry was telling me about it.

EMMA

Jerry? Was he?

ROBERT

He was telling me about it at lunch last week.

EMMA

Really? Does he like it?

ROBERT

Spinks is his boy. He discovered him.

EMMA

Oh. I didn't know that.

ROBERT

Unsolicited manuscript.

Pause.

You think it's good, do you?

EMMA

Yes, I do. I'm enjoying it.

ROBERT

Jerry thinks it's good too. You should have lunch with us one day and chat about it.

EMMA

Is that absolutely necessary?

Pause.

It's not as good as all that.

ROBERT

You mean it's not good enough for you to have lunch with Jerry and me and chat about it?

EMMA

What the hell are you talking about?

ROBERT

I must read it again myself, now it's in hard covers.

EMMA

Again?

ROBERT

Jerry wanted us to publish it.

EMMA

Oh, really?

ROBERT

Well, naturally. Anyway, I turned it down.

EMMA

Why?

ROBERT

Oh . . . not much more to say on that subject, really, is there?

EMMA

What do you consider the subject to be?

ROBERT

Betrayal.

EMMA

No, it isn't.

ROBERT

Isn't it? What is it then?

EMMA

I haven't finished it yet. I'll let you know.

ROBERT

Well, do let me know.

Pause.

Of course, I could be thinking of the wrong book.

Silence.

By the way, I went into American Express yesterday.

She looks up.

EMMA

Oh?

ROBERT

Yes. I went to cash some travellers cheques. You get a much better rate there, you see, than you do in an hotel.

EMMA

Oh, do you?

ROBERT

Oh yes. Anyway, there was a letter there for you. They asked me if you were any relation and I said yes. So they asked me if I wanted to take it. I mean, they gave it to me. But I said no, I would leave it. Did you get it?

EMMA

Yes.

ROBERT

I suppose you popped in when you were out shopping yesterday evening?

EMMA

That's right.

ROBERT

Oh well, I'm glad you got it.

Pause.

To be honest, I was amazed that they suggested I take it. It could never happen in England. But these Italians . . . so free and easy. I mean, just because my name is Downs and your name is Downs doesn't mean that we're the Mr and Mrs Downs that they, in their laughing Mediterranean way, assume we are. We could be, and in fact are vastly more likely to be, total strangers. So let's say I, whom they laughingly assume to be your husband, had taken the letter, having declared myself to be your husband but in truth being a total stranger, and opened it, and read it, out of nothing more than idle curiosity, and then thrown it in a canal, you would never have received it and would have been deprived of your legal right to open your own mail, and all this because of Venetian je m'en foutisme. I've a good mind to write to the Doge of Venice about it.

Pause.

That's what stopped me taking it, by the way, and bringing it to you, the thought that I could very easily be a total stranger.

Pause.

What they of course did not know, and had no way of knowing, was that I am your husband.

EMMA

Pretty inefficient bunch.

ROBERT

Only in a laughing Mediterranean way.

Pause.

EMMA

It was from Jerry.

ROBERT

Yes, I recognised the handwriting.

Pause.

How is he?

EMMA

Okay.

ROBERT

Good. And Judith?

EMMA

Fine.

Pause.

ROBERT

What about the kids?

EMMA

I don't think he mentioned them.

ROBERT

They're probably all right, then. If they were ill or something he'd have probably mentioned it.

Pause.

Any other news?

EMMA

No.

Silence.

ROBERT

Are you looking forward to Torcello?

Pause.

How many times have we been to Torcello? Twice. I remember how you loved it, the first time I took you there. You fell in love with it. That was about ten years ago, wasn't it? About . . . six months after we were married. Yes. Do you remember? I wonder if you'll like it as much tomorrow.

Pause.

What do you think of Jerry as a letter writer?

She laughs shortly.

You're trembling. Are you cold?

EMMA

No.

ROBERT

He used to write to me at one time. Long letters about Ford Madox Ford. I used to write to him too, come to think of it. Long letters about . . . oh, W. B. Yeats, I suppose. That was the time when we were both editors of poetry magazines. Him at Cambridge, me at Oxford. Did you know that? We were bright young men. And close friends. Well, we still are close friends. All that was long before I met you. Long before he met you. I've been trying to remember when I introduced him to you. I simply can't remember. I take it I *did* introduce him to you? Yes. But when? Can you remember?

EMMA

No.

ROBERT

You can't?

EMMA

No.

ROBERT

How odd.

Pause.

He wasn't best man at our wedding, was he?

EMMA

You know he was.

ROBERT

Ah yes. Well, that's probably when I introduced him to you.

Pause.

Was there any message for me, in his letter?

Pause.

I mean in the line of business, to do with the world of publishing. Has he discovered any new and original talent? He's quite talented at uncovering talent, old Jerry.

EMMA

No message.

ROBERT

No message. Not even his love?

Silence.

EMMA

We're lovers.

ROBERT

Ah. Yes. I thought it might be something like that, something along those lines.

EMMA

When?

ROBERT

What?

EMMA

When did you think?

ROBERT

Yesterday. Only yesterday. When I saw his handwriting on the letter. Before yesterday I was quite ignorant.

EMMA

Ah.

Pause.

I'm sorry.

ROBERT

Sorry?

Silence.

Where does it . . . take place? Must be a bit awkward. I mean we've got two kids, he's got two kids, not to mention a wife . . .

EMMA

We have a flat.

ROBERT

Ah. I see.

Pause.

Nice?

Pause.

A flat. It's quite well established then, your . . . uh . . . affair?

EMMA

Yes.

ROBERT

How long?

EMMA

Some time.

ROBERT

Yes, but how long exactly?

EMMA

Five years.

ROBERT

Five years?

Pause.

Ned is one year old.

Pause.

Did you hear what I said?

EMMA

Yes. He's your son. Jerry was in America. For two months.

Silence.

ROBERT

Did he write to you from America?

EMMA

Of course. And I wrote to him.

ROBERT

Did you tell him that Ned had been conceived?

EMMA

Not by letter.

ROBERT

But when you did tell him, was he happy to know I was to be a father?

Pause.

I've always liked Jerry. To be honest, I've always liked him rather more than I've liked you. Maybe I should have had an affair with him myself.

Silence.

Tell me, are you looking forward to our trip to Torcello?

1973 Later

SCENE SIX

Flat. 1973. Summer.

EMMA *and* JERRY *standing, kissing. She is holding a basket and a parcel.*

EMMA

Darling.

JERRY

Darling.

He continues to hold her. She laughs.

EMMA

I must put this down.

She puts basket on table.

JERRY

What's in it?

EMMA

Lunch.

JERRY

What?

EMMA

Things you like.

He pours wine.

How do I look?

JERRY

Beautiful.

EMMA

Do I look well?

JERRY

You do.

He gives her wine.

EMMA (*sipping*)

Mmmnn.

JERRY

How was it?

EMMA

It was lovely.

JERRY

Did you go to Torcello?

EMMA

No.

JERRY

Why not?

EMMA

Oh, I don't know. The speedboats were on strike, or something.

JERRY

On strike?

EMMA

Yes. On the day we were going.

JERRY

Ah. What about the gondolas?

EMMA

You can't take a gondola to Torcello.

JERRY

Well, they used to in the old days, didn't they? Before they had speedboats. How do you think they got over there?

EMMA

It would take hours.

JERRY

Yes. I suppose so.

Pause.

I got your letter.

EMMA

Good.

JERRY

Get mine?

EMMA

Of course. Miss me?

JERRY

Yes. Actually, I haven't been well.

EMMA

What?

JERRY

Oh nothing. A bug.

She kisses him.

EMMA

I missed you.

She turns away, looks about.

You haven't been here . . . at all?

JERRY

No.

EMMA

Needs hoovering.

JERRY

Later.

Pause.

I spoke to Robert this morning.

EMMA

Oh?

JERRY

I'm taking him to lunch on Thursday.

EMMA

Thursday? Why?

JERRY

Well, it's my turn.

EMMA

No, I meant why are you taking him to lunch?

JERRY

Because it's my turn. Last time he took me to lunch.

EMMA

You know what I mean.

JERRY

No. What?

EMMA

What is the subject or point of your lunch?

JERRY

No subject or point. We've just been doing it for years. His turn, followed by my turn.

EMMA

You've misunderstood me.

JERRY

Have I? How?

EMMA

Well, quite simply, you often do meet, or have lunch, to discuss a particular writer or a particular book, don't you? So to those meetings, or lunches, there is a point or a subject.

JERRY

Well, there isn't to this one.

Pause.

EMMA

You haven't discovered any new writers, while I've been away?

JERRY

No. Sam fell off his bike.

EMMA

No.

JERRY

He was knocked out. He was out for about a minute.

EMMA

Were you with him?

JERRY

No. Judith. He's all right. And then I got this bug.

EMMA

Oh dear.

JERRY

So I've had time for nothing.

EMMA

Everything will be better, now I'm back.

JERRY

Yes.

EMMA

Oh, I read that Spinks, the book you gave me.

JERRY

What do you think?

EMMA

Excellent.

JERRY

Robert hated it. He wouldn't publish it.

EMMA

What's he like?

JERRY

Who?

EMMA

Spinks.

JERRY

Spinks? He's a very thin bloke. About fifty. Wears dark glasses day and night. He lives alone, in a furnished room. Quite like this one, actually. He's . . . unfussed.

EMMA

Furnished rooms suit him?

JERRY

Yes.

EMMA

They suit me too. And you? Do you still like it? Our home?

JERRY

It's marvellous not to have a telephone.

EMMA

And marvellous to have me?

JERRY

You're all right.

EMMA

I cook and slave for you.

JERRY

You do.

EMMA

I bought something in Venice – for the house.

She opens the parcel, takes out a tablecloth. Puts it on the table.

Do you like it?

JERRY

It's lovely.

Pause.

EMMA

Do you think we'll ever go to Venice together?

Pause.

No. Probably not.

Pause.

JERRY

You don't think I should see Robert for lunch on Thursday, or on Friday, for that matter?

EMMA

Why do you say that?

JERRY

You don't think I should see him at all?

EMMA

I didn't say that. How can you not see him? Don't be silly.

Pause.

JERRY

I had a terrible panic when you were away. I was sorting out a contract, in my office, with some lawyers. I suddenly couldn't remember what I'd done with your letter. I couldn't remember putting it in the safe. I said I had to look for something in the safe. I opened the safe. It wasn't there. I had to go on with the damn contract . . . I kept seeing it lying somewhere in the house, being picked up . . .

EMMA

Did you find it?

JERRY

It was in the pocket of a jacket – in my wardrobe – at home.

EMMA

God.

JERRY

Something else happened a few months ago – I didn't tell you. We had a drink one evening. Well, we had our drink, and I got home about eight, walked in the door,

Judith said, hello, you're a bit late. Sorry, I said, I was having a drink with Spinks. Spinks? she said, how odd, he's just phoned, five minutes ago, wanted to speak to you, he didn't mention he'd just seen you. You know old Spinks, I said, not exactly forthcoming, is he? He'd probably remembered something he'd meant to say but hadn't. I'll ring him later. I went up to see the kids and then we all had dinner.

Pause.

Listen. Do you remember, when was it, a few years ago, we were all in your kitchen, must have been Christmas or something, do you remember, all the kids were running about and suddenly I picked Charlotte up and lifted her high up, high up, and then down and up. Do you remember how she laughed?

EMMA

Everyone laughed.

JERRY

She was so light. And there was your husband and my wife and all the kids, all standing and laughing in your kitchen. I can't get rid of it.

EMMA

It was your kitchen, actually.

He takes her hand. They stand. They go to the bed and lie down.

Why shouldn't you throw her up?

She caresses him. They embrace.

1973 Later

SCENE SEVEN

Restaurant. 1973. Summer.

ROBERT *at table drinking white wine. The* WAITER *brings* JERRY *to the table.* JERRY *sits.*

JERRY

Hullo, Robert.

ROBERT

Hullo.

JERRY (*to the* WAITER)

I'd like a Scotch on the rocks.

WAITER

With water?

JERRY

What?

WAITER

You want it with water?

JERRY

No. No water. Just on the rocks.

WAITER

Certainly signore.

ROBERT

Scotch? You don't usually drink Scotch at lunchtime.

JERRY

I've had a bug, actually.

ROBERT

Ah.

JERRY

And the only thing to get rid of this bug was Scotch – at lunchtime as well as at night. So I'm still drinking Scotch at lunchtime in case it comes back.

ROBERT

Like an apple a day.

JERRY

Precisely.

WAITER *brings Scotch on rocks.*

Cheers.

ROBERT

Cheers.

WAITER

The menus, signori.

He passes the menus, goes.

ROBERT

How are you? Apart from the bug?

JERRY

Fine.

ROBERT

Ready for some squash?

JERRY

When I've got rid of the bug, yes.

ROBERT

I thought you had got rid of it.

JERRY

Why do you think I'm still drinking Scotch at lunchtime?

ROBERT

Oh yes. We really must play. We haven't played for years.

JERRY

How old are you now, then?

ROBERT

Thirty-six.

JERRY

That means I'm thirty-six as well.

ROBERT

If you're a day.

JERRY

Bit violent, squash.

ROBERT

Ring me. We'll have a game.

JERRY

How was Venice?

WAITER

Ready to order, signori?

ROBERT

What'll you have?

JERRY *looks at him, briefly, then back to the menu.*

JERRY

I'll have melone. And Piccata al limone with a green salad.

WAITER

Insalate verde. Prosciutto e melone?

JERRY

No. Just melone. On the rocks.

ROBERT

I'll have prosciutto and melone. Fried scampi. And spinach.

WAITER

E spinaci. Grazie, signore.

ROBERT

And a bottle of Corvo Bianco straight away.

WAITER

Si, signore. Molte grazies. (*He goes.*)

JERRY

Is he the one who's always been here or is it his son?

ROBERT

You mean has his son always been here?

JERRY

No, is *he* his son? I mean, is he the son of the one who's always been here?

ROBERT

No, he's his father.

JERRY

Ah. Is he?

ROBERT

He's the one who speaks wonderful Italian.

JERRY

Yes. Your Italian's pretty good, isn't it?

ROBERT

No. Not at all.

JERRY

Yes it is.

ROBERT

No, it's Emma's Italian which is very good. Emma's Italian is very good.

JERRY

Is it? I didn't know that.

WAITER *with bottle.*

WAITER

Corvo Bianco, signore.

ROBERT

Thank you.

JERRY

How was it, anyway? Venice.

WAITER

Venice, signore? Beautiful. A most beautiful place of Italy. You see that painting on the wall? Is Venice.

ROBERT

So it is.

WAITER

You know what is none of in Venice?

JERRY

What?

WAITER

Traffico.

He goes, smiling.

ROBERT

Cheers.

JERRY

Cheers.

ROBERT

When were you last there?

JERRY

Oh, years.

ROBERT

How's Judith?

JERRY

What? Oh, you know, okay. Busy.

ROBERT

And the kids?

JERRY

All right. Sam fell off –

ROBERT

What?

JERRY

No, no, nothing. So how was it?

ROBERT

You used to go there with Judith, didn't you?

JERRY

Yes, but we haven't been there for years.

Pause.

How about Charlotte? Did she enjoy it?

ROBERT

I think she did.

Pause.

I did.

JERRY

Good.

ROBERT

I went for a trip to Torcello.

JERRY

Oh, really? Lovely place.

ROBERT

Incredible day. I got up very early and – whoomp – right across the lagoon – to Torcello. Not a soul stirring.

JERRY

What's the 'whoomp'?

ROBERT

Speedboat.

JERRY

Ah. I thought –

ROBERT

What?

JERRY

It's so long ago, I'm obviously wrong. I thought one went to Torcello by gondola.

ROBERT

It would take hours. No, no, – whoomp – across the lagoon in the dawn.

JERRY

Sounds good.

ROBERT

I was quite alone.

JERRY

Where was Emma?

ROBERT

I think asleep.

JERRY

Ah.

ROBERT

I was alone for hours, as a matter of fact, on the island. Highpoint, actually, of the whole trip.

JERRY

Was it? Well, it sounds marvellous.

ROBERT

Yes. I sat on the grass and read Yeats.

JERRY

Yeats on Torcello?

ROBERT

They went well together.

WAITER *with food.*

WAITER

One melone. One prosciutto e melone.

ROBERT

Prosciutto for me.

WAITER

Buon appetito.

ROBERT

Emma read that novel of that chum of yours – what's his name?

JERRY

I don't know. What?

ROBERT

Spinks.

JERRY

Oh Spinks. Yes. The one you didn't like.

ROBERT

The one I wouldn't publish.

JERRY

I remember. Did Emma like it?

ROBERT

She seemed to be madly in love with it.

JERRY

Good.

ROBERT

You like it yourself, do you?

JERRY

I do.

ROBERT

And it's very successful?

JERRY

It is.

ROBERT

Tell me, do you think that makes me a publisher of unique critical judgement or a foolish publisher?

JERRY

A foolish publisher.

ROBERT

I agree with you. I am a very foolish publisher.

JERRY

No you're not. What are you talking about? You're a good publisher. What are you talking about?

ROBERT

I'm a bad publisher because I hate books. Or to be more precise, prose. Or to be even more precise, modern prose, I mean modern novels, first novels and second novels, all that promise and sensibility it falls upon me to judge, to put the firm's money on, and then to push for the third novel, see it done, see the dust jacket done, see the dinner for the national literary editors done, see the signing in Hatchards done, see the lucky author cook himself to death, all in the name of literature. You know what you and Emma have in common? You love literature. I mean you love modern prose literature, I mean you love the new novel by the new Casey or Spinks. It gives you both a thrill.

JERRY

You must be pissed.

ROBERT

Really? You mean you don't think it gives Emma a thrill?

JERRY

How do I know? She's your wife.

Pause.

ROBERT

Yes. Yes. You're quite right. I shouldn't have to consult you. I shouldn't have to consult anyone.

JERRY

I'd like some more wine.

ROBERT

Yes, yes. Waiter! Another bottle of Corvo Bianco. And where's our lunch? This place is going to pot. Mind you, it's worse in Venice. They really don't give a fuck there. I'm not drunk. You can't get drunk on Corvo Bianco. Mind you . . . last night . . . I was up late . . . I hate brandy . . . it stinks of modern literature. No, look, I'm sorry . . .

WAITER *with bottle.*

WAITER

Corvo Bianco.

ROBERT

Same glass. Where's our lunch?

WAITER

It comes.

ROBERT

I'll pour.

WAITER *goes, with melon plates.*

No, look, I'm sorry, have another drink. I'll tell you what it is, it's just that I can't bear being back in London. I was happy, such a rare thing, not in Venice, I don't mean that, I mean on Torcello, when I walked about Torcello in the early morning, alone, I was happy, I wanted to stay there for ever.

JERRY

We all . . .

ROBERT

Yes, we all . . . feel that sometimes. Oh you do yourself, do you?

Pause.

I mean there's nothing really wrong, you see. I've got the family. Emma and I are very good together. I think the world of her. And I actually consider Casey to be a first-rate writer.

JERRY

Do you really?

ROBERT

First rate. I'm proud to publish him and you discovered him and that was very clever of you.

JERRY

Thanks.

ROBERT

You've got a good nose and you care and I respect that in you. So does Emma. We often talk about it.

JERRY

How is Emma?

ROBERT

Very well. You must come and have a drink sometime. She'd love to see you.

1971

SCENE EIGHT

Flat. 1971. Summer.

Flat empty. Kitchen door open. Table set; crockery, glasses, bottle of wine.

JERRY *comes in through front door, with key.*

JERRY

Hullo.

EMMA*'s voice from kitchen.*

EMMA

Hullo.

EMMA *comes out of kitchen. She is wearing an apron.*

EMMA

I've only just got here. I meant to be here ages ago. I'm making this stew. It'll be hours.

He kisses her.

Are you starving?

JERRY

Yes.

He kisses her.

EMMA

No really. I'll never do it. You sit down. I'll get it on.

JERRY

What a lovely apron.

EMMA

Good.

She kisses him, goes into kitchen.
She calls. He pours wine.

EMMA

What have you been doing?

JERRY

Just walked through the park.

EMMA

What was it like?

JERRY

Beautiful. Empty. A slight mist.

Pause.

I sat down for a bit, under a tree. It was very quiet. I just looked at the Serpentine.

Pause.

EMMA

And then?

JERRY

Then I got a taxi to Wessex Grove. Number 31. And I climbed the steps and opened the front door and then climbed the stairs and opened this door and found you in a new apron cooking a stew.

EMMA *comes out of the kitchen.*

EMMA

It's on.

JERRY

Which is now on.

EMMA *pours herself a vodka.*

JERRY

Vodka? At lunchtime?

EMMA

Just feel like one.

She drinks.

I ran into Judith yesterday. Did she tell you?

JERRY

No, she didn't.

Pause.

Where?

EMMA

Lunch.

JERRY

Lunch?

EMMA

She didn't tell you?

JERRY

No.

EMMA

That's funny.

JERRY

What do you mean, lunch? Where?

EMMA

At Gino's.

JERRY

Gino's? What the hell was she doing at Gino's?

EMMA

Having lunch. With a woman.

JERRY

A woman?

EMMA

Yes.

Pause.

JERRY

Gino's is a long way from the hospital.

EMMA

Of course it isn't.

JERRY

Well . . . I suppose not.

Pause.

And you?

EMMA

Me?

JERRY

What were you doing at Gino's ?

EMMA

Having lunch with my sister.

JERRY

Ah.

Pause.

EMMA

Judith . . . didn't tell you?

JERRY

I haven't really seen her. I was out late last night, with Casey. And she was out early this morning.

Pause.

EMMA

Do you think she knows?

JERRY

Knows?

EMMA

Does she know? About us?

JERRY

No.

EMMA

Are you sure?

JERRY

She's too busy. At the hospital. And then the kids. She doesn't go in for . . . speculation.

EMMA

But what about clues? Isn't she interested . . . to follow clues?

JERRY

What clues?

EMMA

Well, there must be some . . . available to her . . . to pick up.

JERRY

There are none . . . available to her.

EMMA

Oh. Well . . . good.

JERRY

She has an admirer.

EMMA

Really?

JERRY

Another doctor. He takes her for drinks. It's . . . irritating. I mean, she says that's all there is to it. He likes her, she's fond of him, et cetera, et cetera . . . perhaps that's what I find irritating. I don't know exactly what's going on.

EMMA

Oh, why shouldn't she have an admirer? I have an admirer.

JERRY

Who?

EMMA

Uuh . . . you, I think.

JERRY

Ah. Yes.

He takes her hand.

I'm more than that.

Pause.

EMMA

Tell me . . . have you ever thought . . . of changing your life?

JERRY

Changing?

EMMA

Mmnn.

Pause.

JERRY

It's impossible.

Pause.

EMMA

Do you think she's being unfaithful to you?

JERRY

No. I don't know.

EMMA

When you were in America, just now, for instance?

JERRY

No.

EMMA

Have you ever been unfaithful?

JERRY

To whom?

EMMA

To me, of course.

JERRY

No.

Pause.

Have you . . . to me?

EMMA

No.

Pause.

If she was, what would you do?

JERRY

She isn't. She's busy. She's got lots to do. She's a very good doctor. She likes her life. She loves the kids.

EMMA

Ah.

JERRY

She loves me.

Pause.

EMMA

Ah.

Silence.

JERRY

All that means something.

EMMA

It certainly does.

JERRY

But I adore you.

Pause.

I adore you.

EMMA *takes his hand.*

EMMA

Yes.

Pause.

Listen. There's something I have to tell you.

JERRY

What?

EMMA

I'm pregnant. It was when you were in America.

Pause.

It wasn't anyone else. It was my husband.

Pause.

JERRY

Yes. Yes, of course.

Pause.

I'm very happy for you.

1968

SCENE NINE

Robert and Emma's House. Bedroom. 1968. Winter.

The room is dimly lit. JERRY *is sitting in the shadows. Faint music through the door.*

The door opens. Light. Music. EMMA *comes in, closes the door. She goes towards the mirror, sees* JERRY.

EMMA

Good God.

JERRY

I've been waiting for you.

EMMA

What do you mean?

JERRY

I knew you'd come.

He drinks.

EMMA

I've just come in to comb my hair.

He stands.

JERRY

I knew you'd have to. I knew you'd have to comb your

hair. I knew you'd have to get away from the party.

She goes to the mirror, combs her hair.
He watches her.

You're a beautiful hostess.

EMMA

Aren't you enjoying the party?

JERRY

You're beautiful.

He goes to her.

Listen. I've been watching you all night. I must tell you, I want to tell you, I have to tell you –

EMMA

Please –

JERRY

You're incredible.

EMMA

You're drunk.

JERRY

Nevertheless.

He holds her.

EMMA

Jerry.

JERRY

I was best man at your wedding. I saw you in white. I watched you glide by in white.

EMMA

I wasn't in white.

JERRY

You know what should have happened?

EMMA

What?

JERRY

I should have had you, in your white, before the wedding. I should have blackened you, in your white wedding dress, blackened you in your bridal dress, before ushering you into your wedding, as your best man.

EMMA

My husband's best man. Your best friend's best man.

JERRY

No. Your best man.

EMMA

I must get back.

JERRY

You're lovely. I'm crazy about you. All these words I'm using, don't you see, they've never been said before. Can't you see? I'm crazy about you. It's a whirlwind. Have you ever been to the Sahara Desert? Listen to me. It's true. Listen. You overwhelm me. You're so lovely.

EMMA

I'm not.

JERRY

You're so beautiful. Look at the way you look at me.

EMMA

I'm not . . . looking at you.

JERRY

Look at the way you're looking at me. I can't wait for you, I'm bowled over, I'm totally knocked out, you dazzle me, you jewel, my jewel, I can't ever sleep again, no, listen, it's the truth, I won't walk, I'll be a cripple, I'll descend, I'll diminish, into total paralysis, my life is in your hands, that's what you're banishing me to, a state of catatonia, do you know the state of catatonia? do you? do you? the state of . . . where the reigning prince is the prince of emptiness, the prince of absence, the prince of desolation. I love you.

EMMA

My husband is at the other side of that door.

JERRY

Everyone knows. The world knows. It knows. But

they'll never know, they'll never know, they're in a different world. I adore you. I'm madly in love with you. I can't believe that what anyone is at this moment saying has ever happened has ever happened. Nothing has ever happened. Nothing. This is the only thing that has ever happened. Your eyes kill me. I'm lost. You're wonderful.

EMMA

No.

JERRY

Yes.

He kisses her.
She breaks away.
He kisses her.

Laughter off.
She breaks away.
Door opens. ROBERT.

EMMA

Your best friend is drunk.

JERRY

As you are my best and oldest friend and, in the present instance, my host, I decided to take this opportunity to tell your wife how beautiful she was.

ROBERT

Quite right.

JERRY

It is quite right, to . . . to face up to the facts . . . and to offer a token, without blush, a token of one's unalloyed appreciation, no holds barred.

ROBERT

Absolutely.

JERRY

And how wonderful for you that this is so, that this is the case, that her beauty is the case.

ROBERT

Quite right.

JERRY *moves to* ROBERT *and take hold of his elbow.*

JERRY

I speak as your oldest friend. Your best man.

ROBERT

You are, actually.

He clasps JERRY*'s shoulder, briefly, turns, leaves the room.*

EMMA *moves towards the door.* JERRY *grasps her arm. She stops still.*

They stand still, looking at each other.

ff

Faber Modern Classics was launched in April 2015 and draws upon Faber & Faber's unique and diverse publishing since the company was first established in 1929. With titles from the fiction, non-fiction, poetry and drama lists brought together in one beautiful livery, these are the books and authors that have earned Faber a reputation for publishing the most powerful and original writing of each generation.